Kay and Aiden

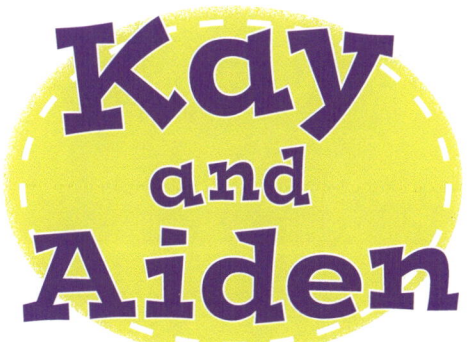

The Tram Bell

Kay and Aiden

The Tram Bell

Written by Carol Mitchell

Illustrated by Alan Brown

Collins

Chapter 1

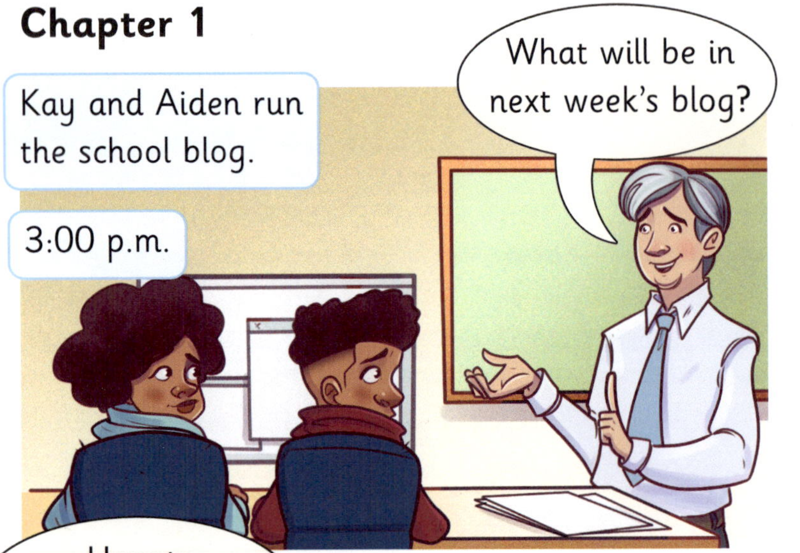

Kay and Aiden run the school blog.
3:00 p.m.
What will be in next week's blog?

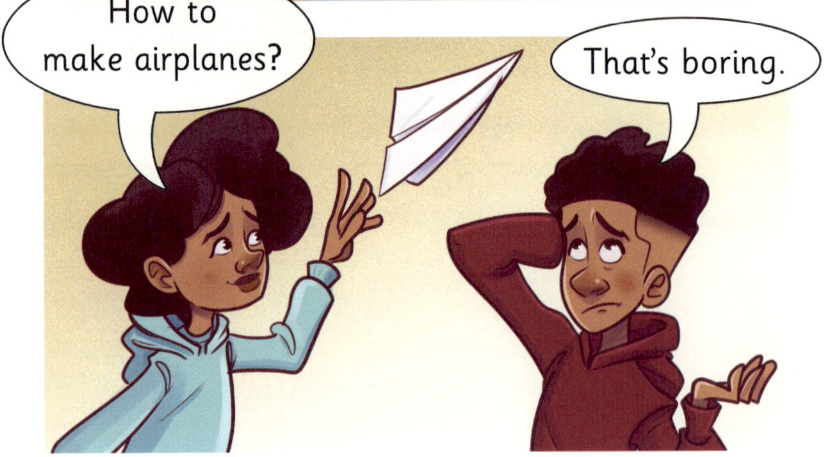

How to make airplanes?
That's boring.

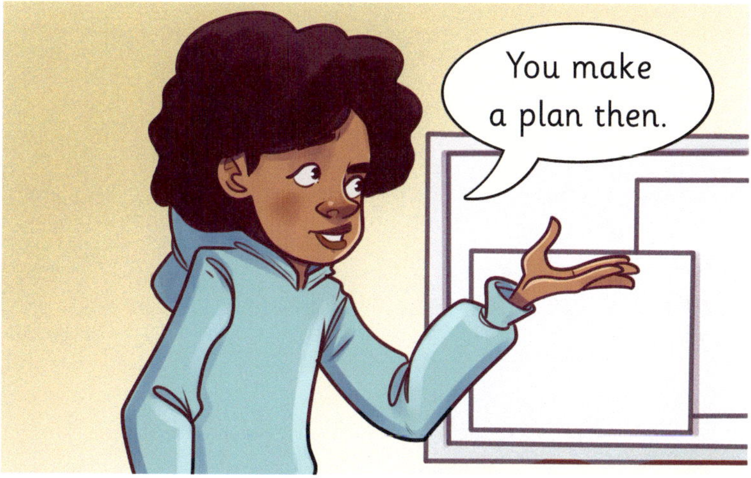
You make a plan then.

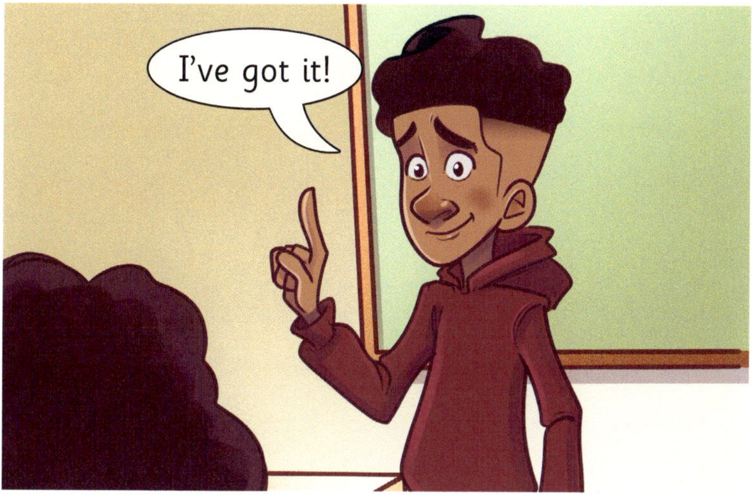
I've got it!

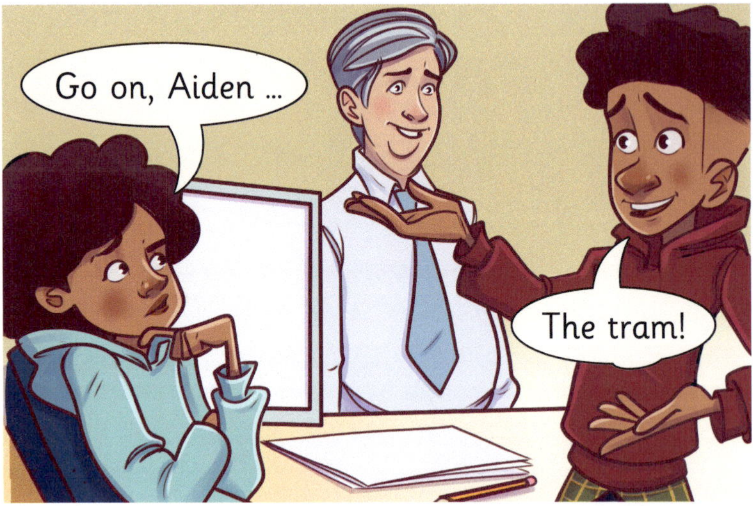
Go on, Aiden ...
The tram!

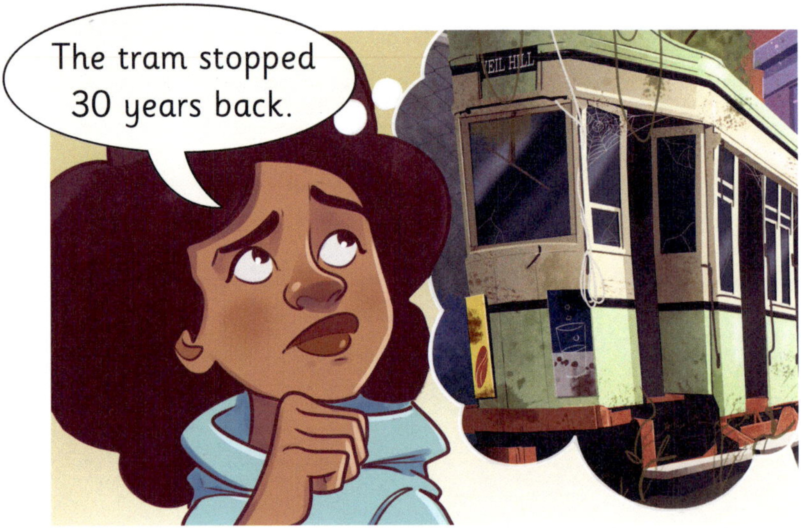
The tram stopped
30 years back.
VEIL HILL

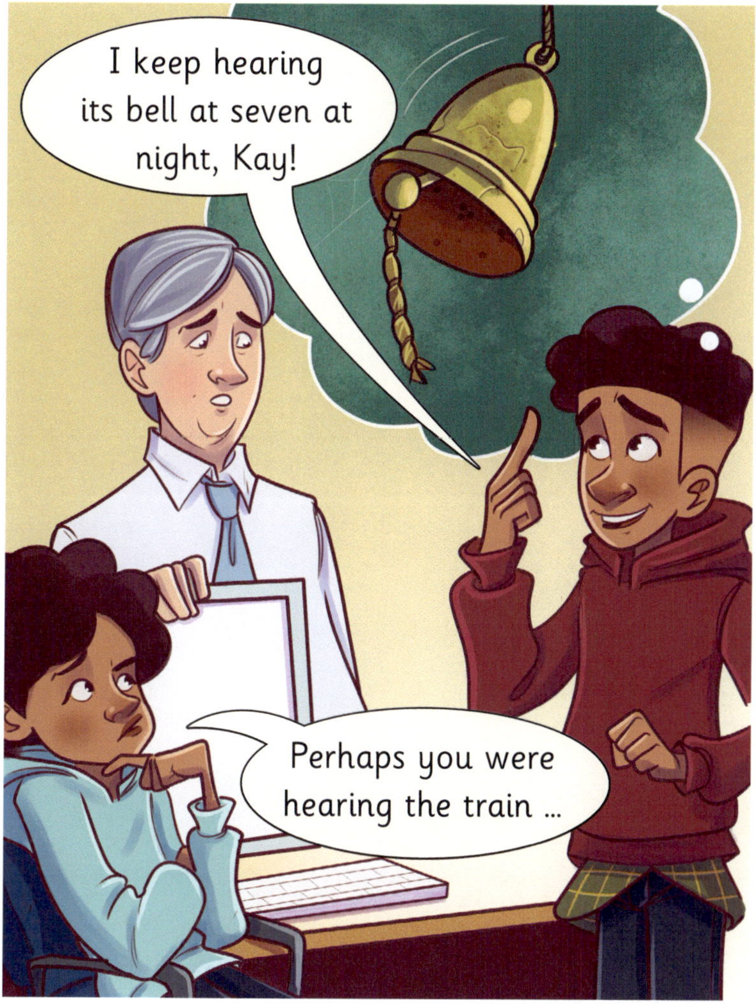
I keep hearing its bell at seven at night, Kay!
Perhaps you were hearing the train ...

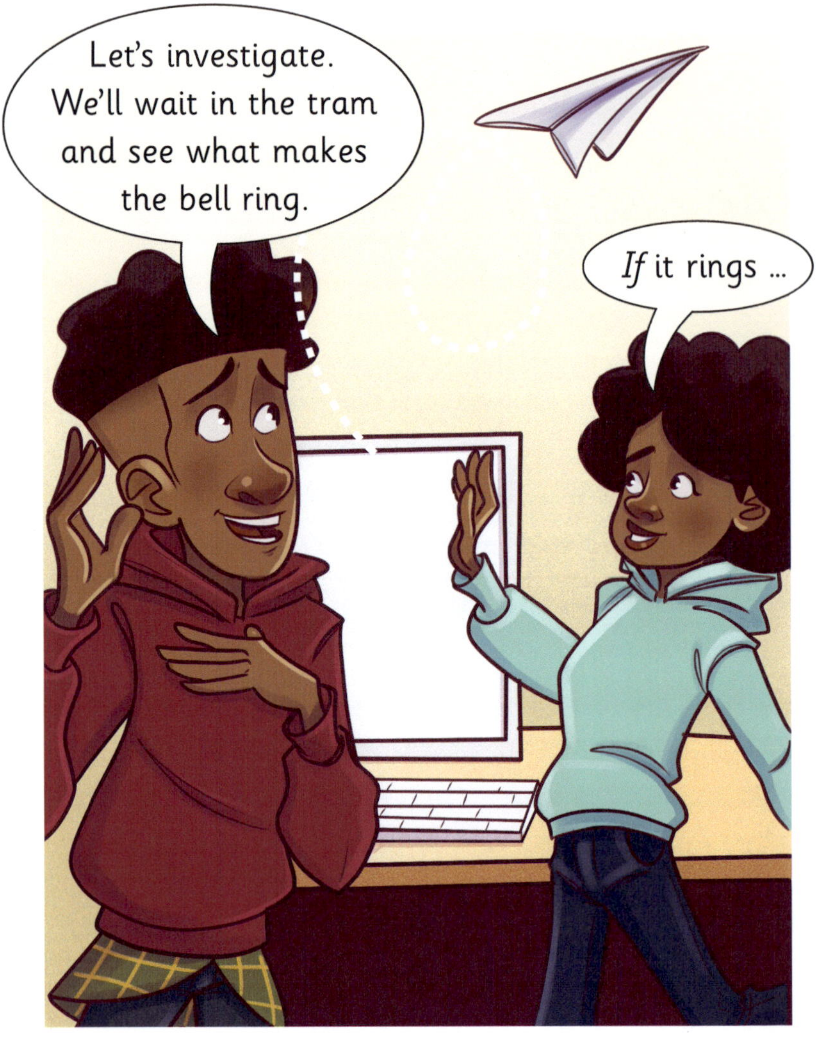
Let's investigate. We'll wait in the tram and see what makes the bell ring.
If it rings ...

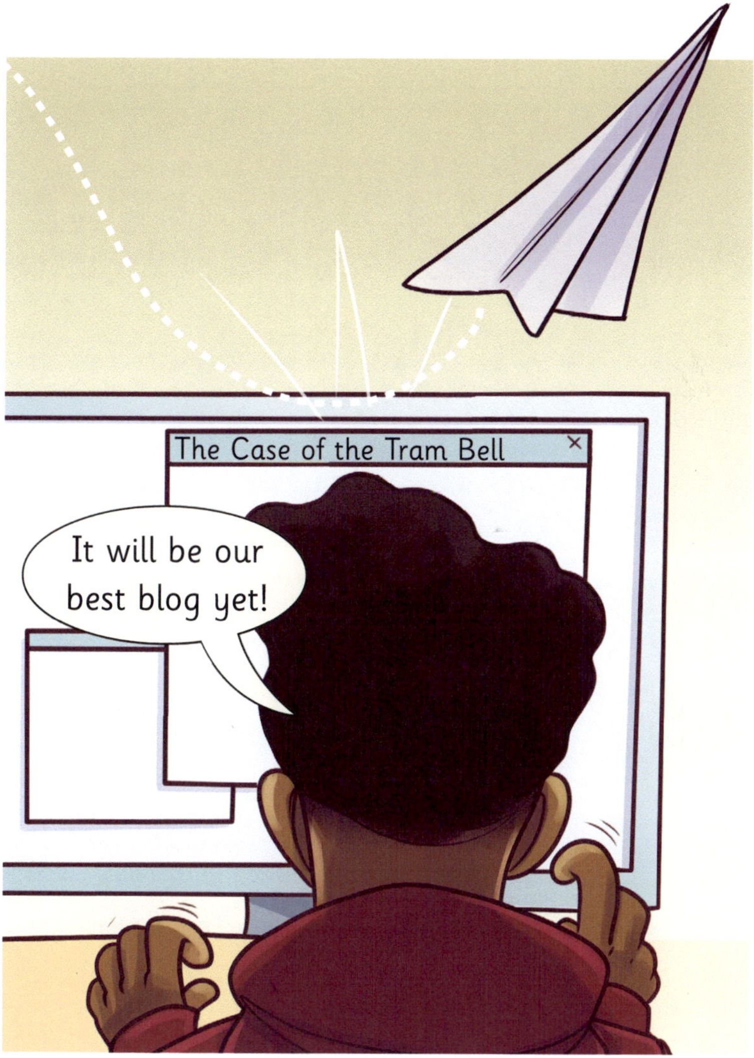
The Case of the Tram Bell
It will be our best blog yet!

Chapter 2

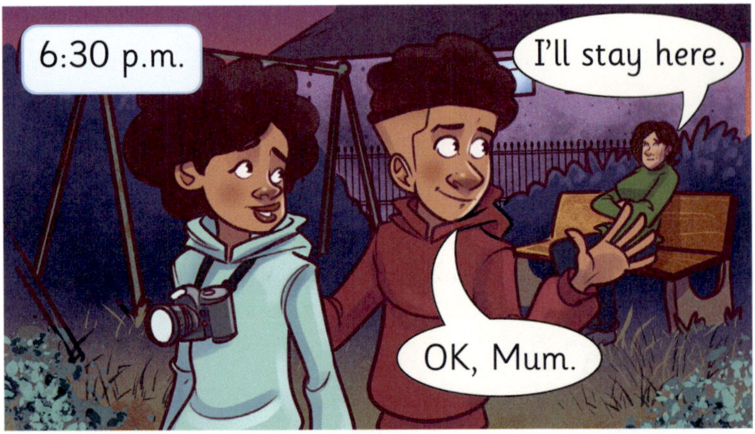
6:30 p.m.
I'll stay here.
OK, Mum.

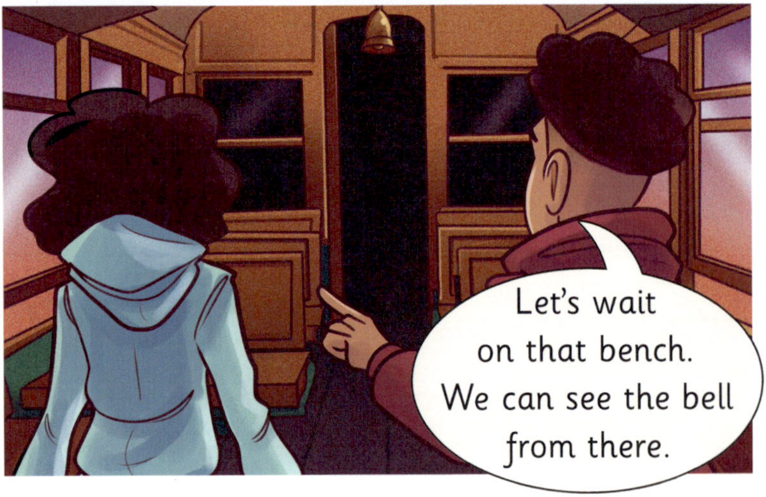
Let's wait on that bench. We can see the bell from there.

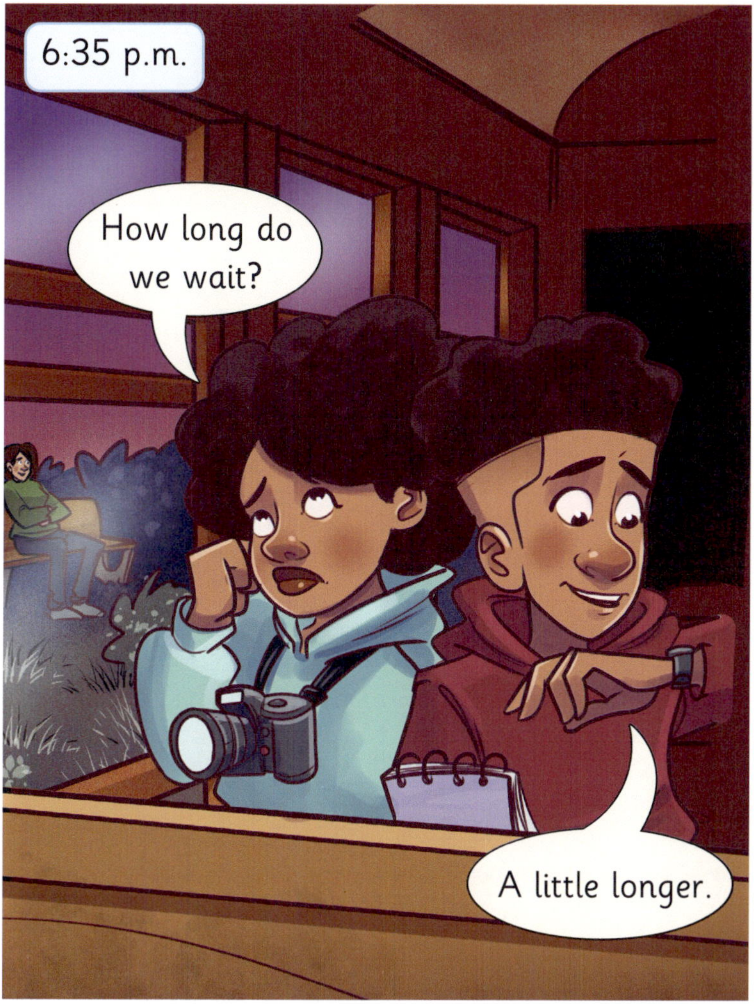
6:35 p.m.
How long do we wait?
A little longer.

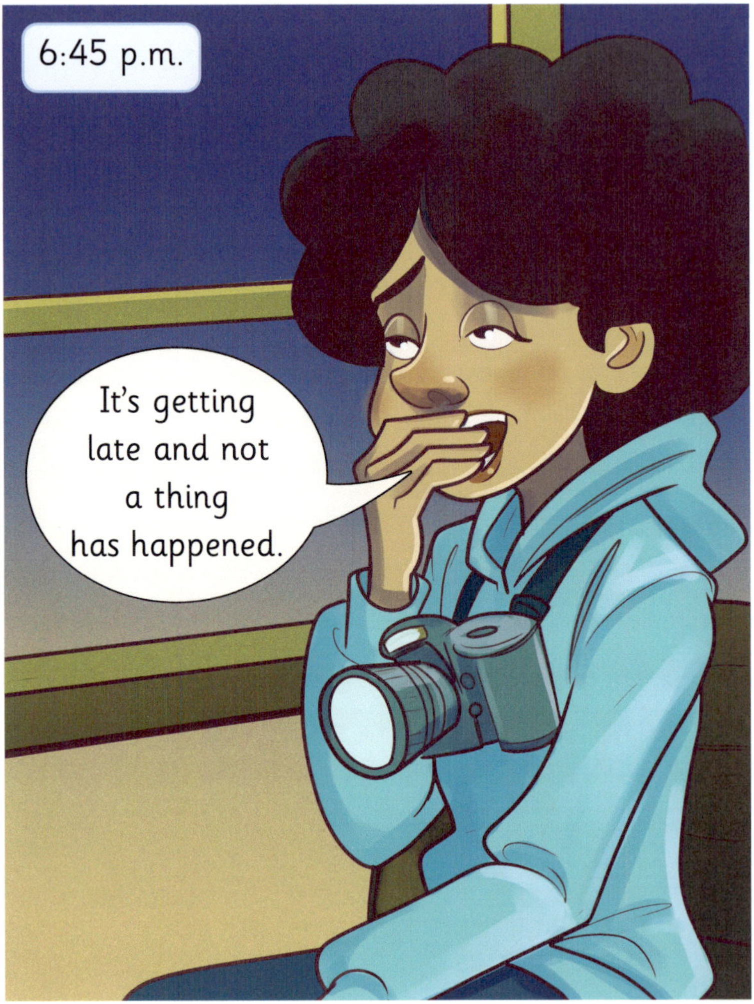
6:45 p.m.
It's getting late and not a thing has happened.

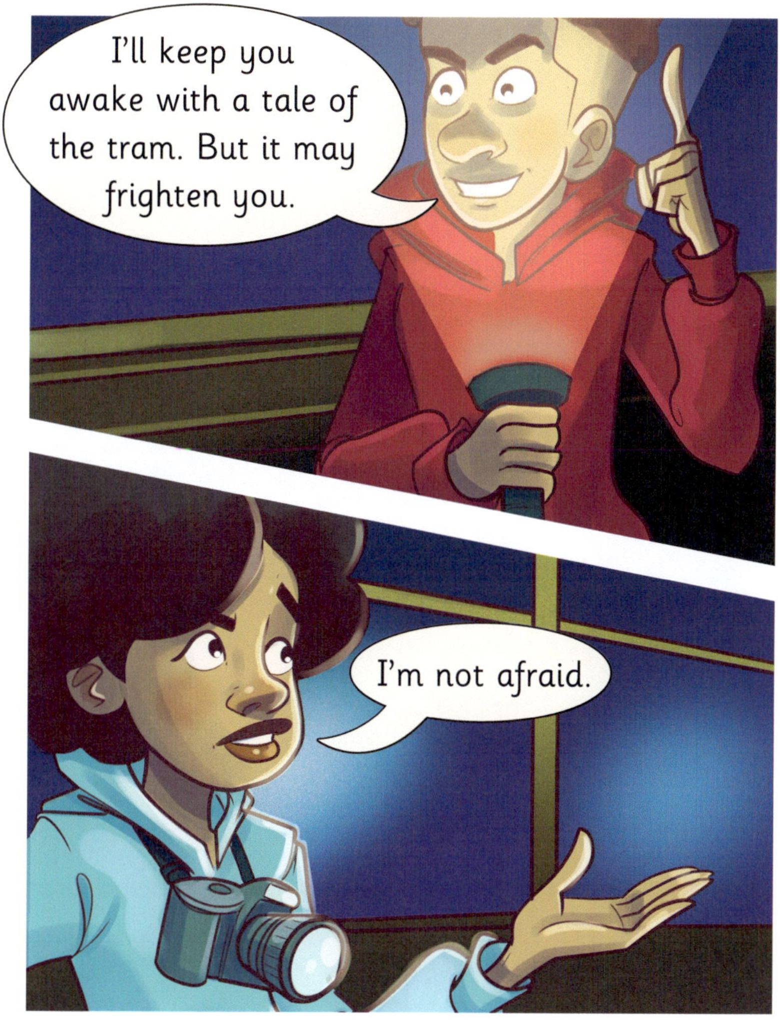
I'll keep you awake with a tale of the tram. But it may frighten you.
I'm not afraid.

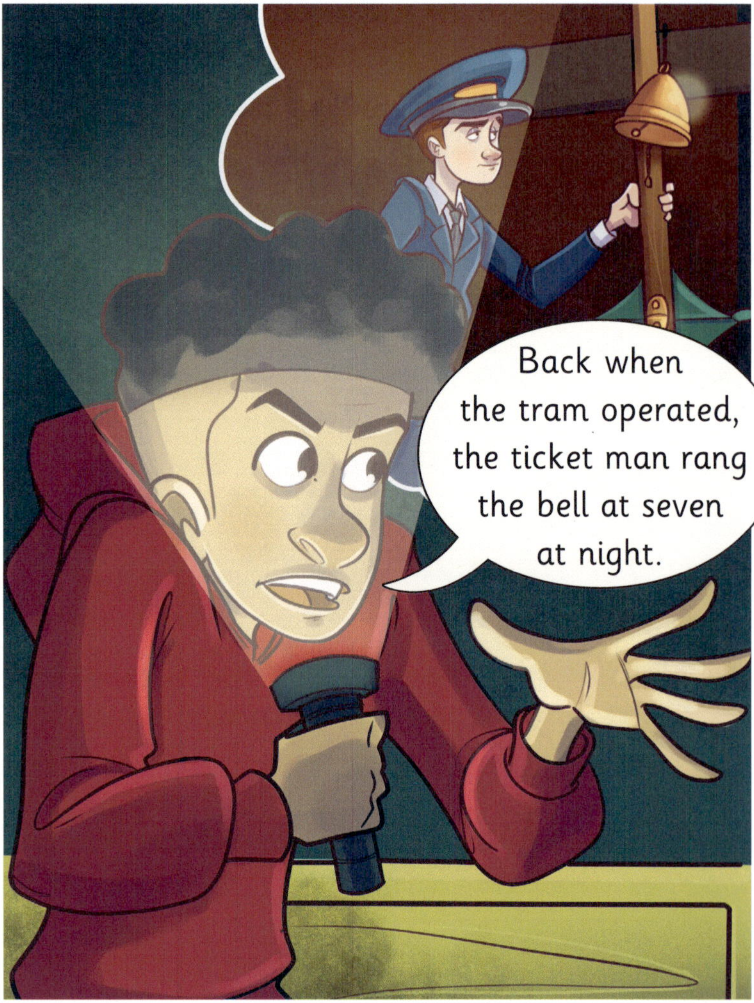
Back when the tram operated, the ticket man rang the bell at seven at night.

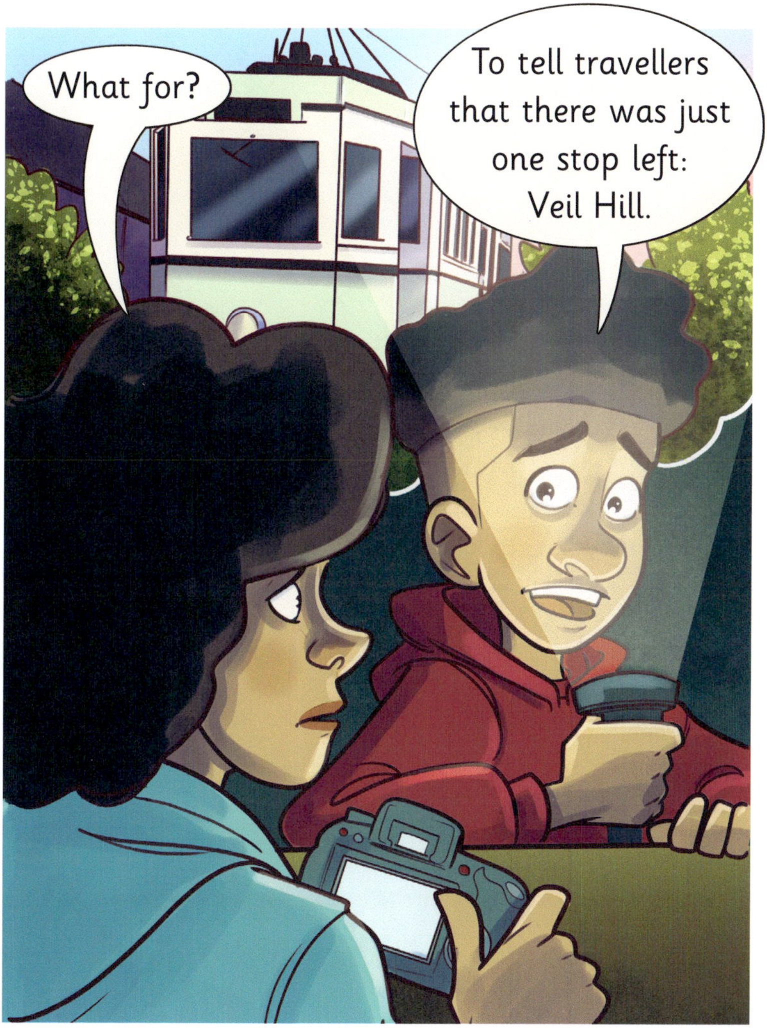
What for?
To tell travellers that there was just one stop left: Veil Hill.

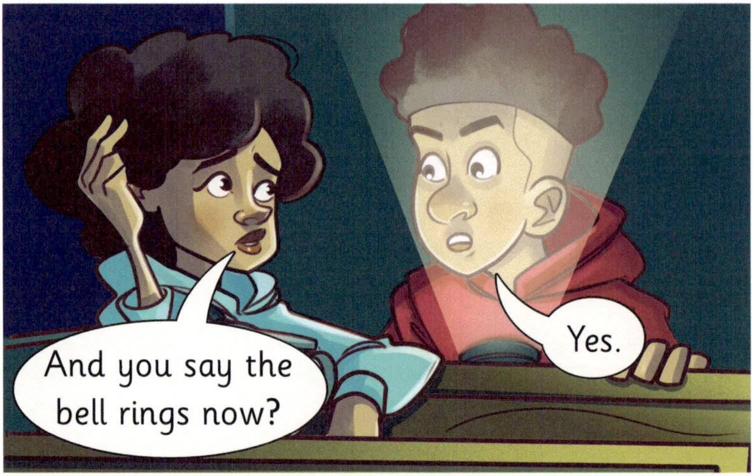
And you say the bell rings now?
Yes.

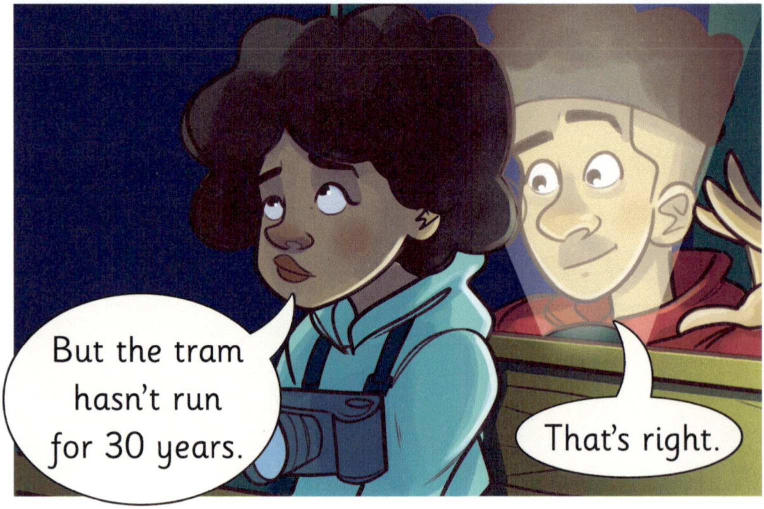
But the tram hasn't run for 30 years.
That's right.

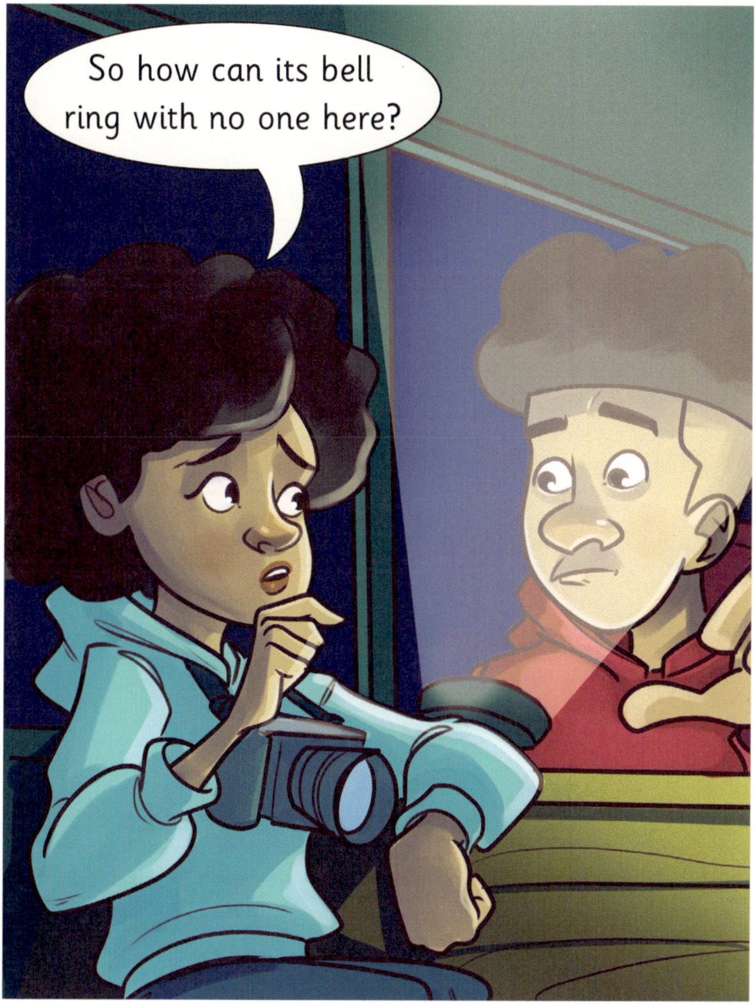
So how can its bell ring with no one here?

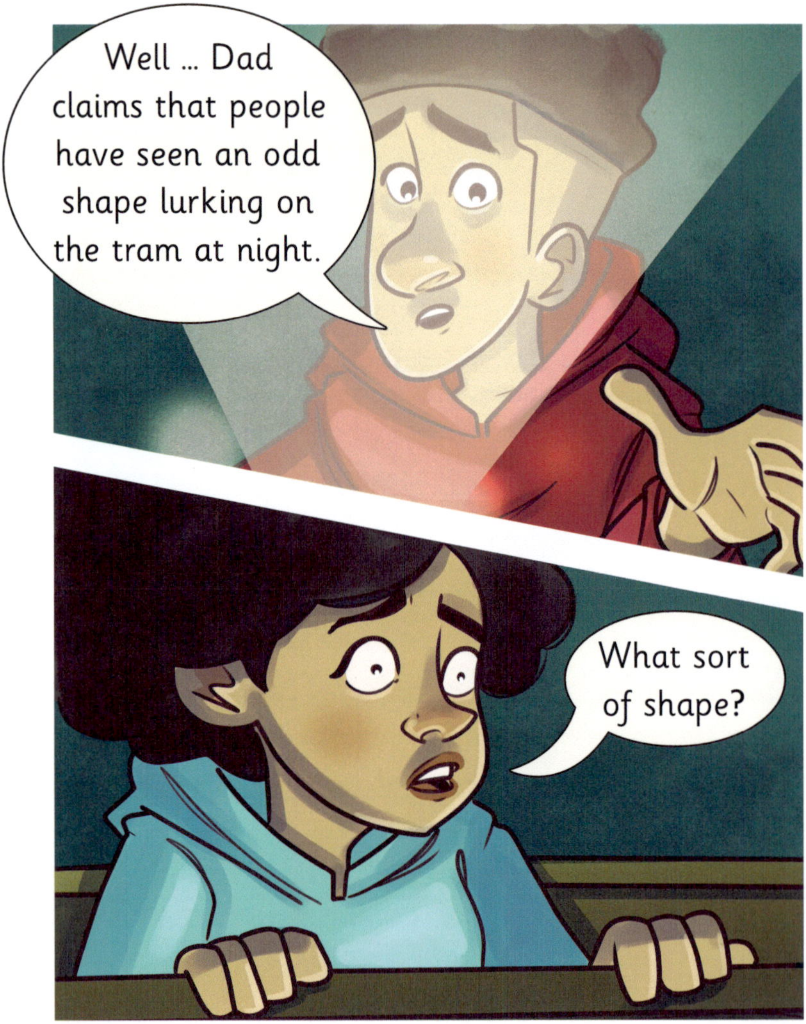
Well ... Dad claims that people have seen an odd shape lurking on the tram at night.
What sort of shape?

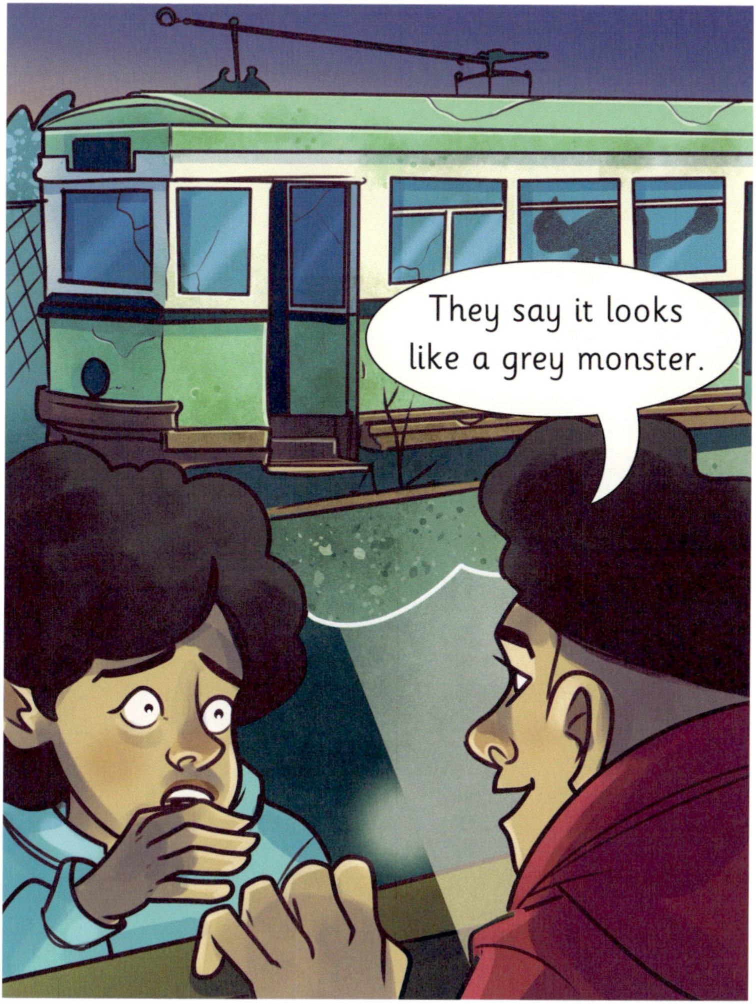
They say it looks like a grey monster.

Chapter 3

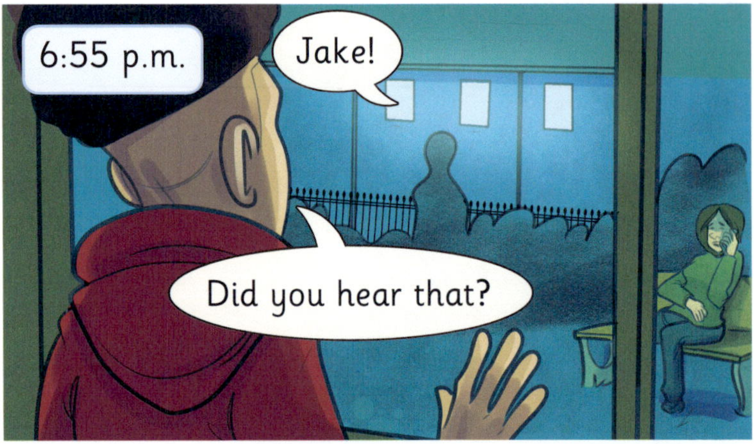
6:55 p.m.
Jake!
Did you hear that?

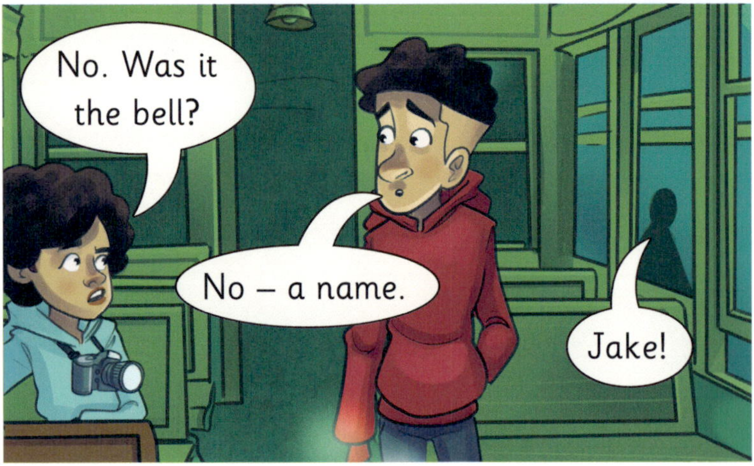
No. Was it the bell?
No – a name.
Jake!

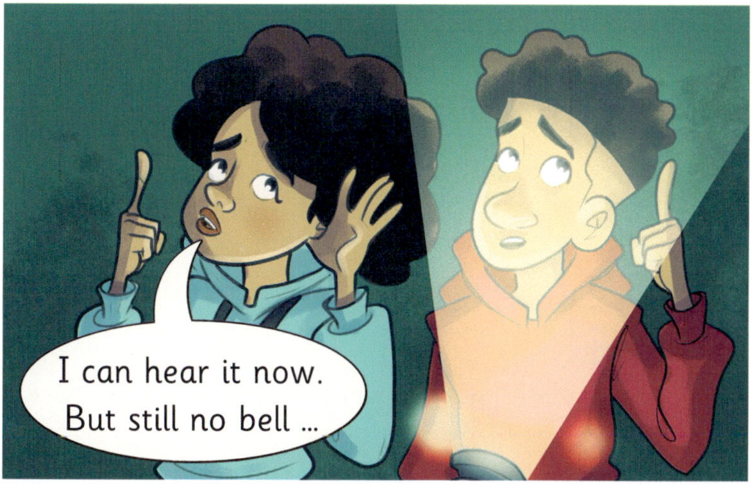
I can hear it now.
But still no bell ...

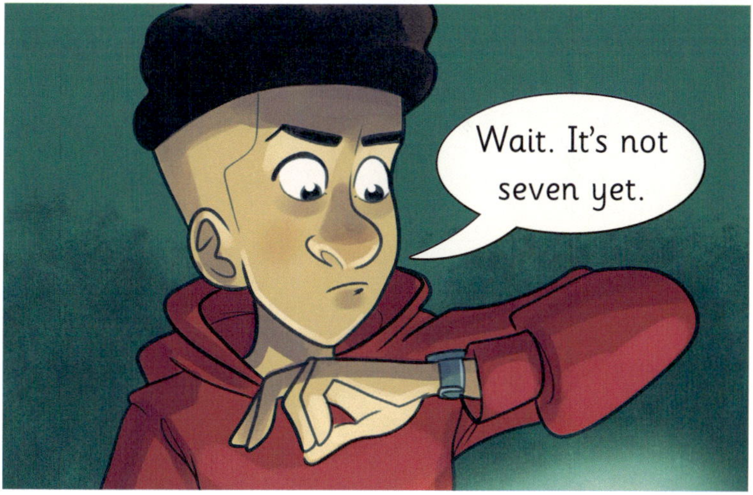
Wait. It's not
seven yet.

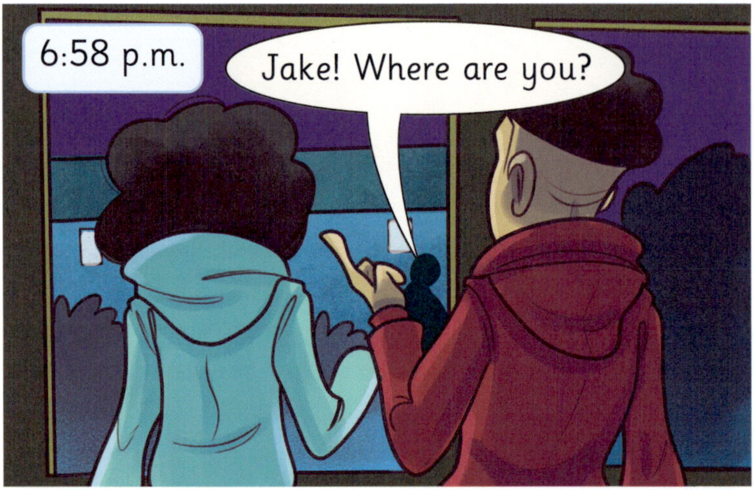
6:58 p.m.
Jake! Where are you?

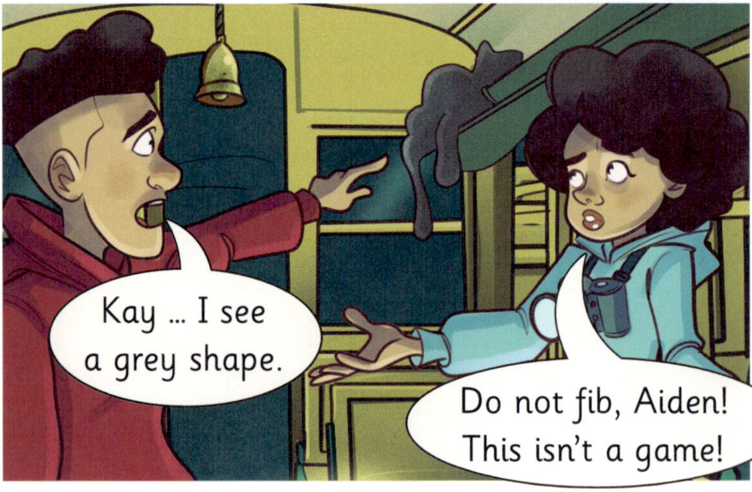
Kay … I see a grey shape.
Do not fib, Aiden! This isn't a game!

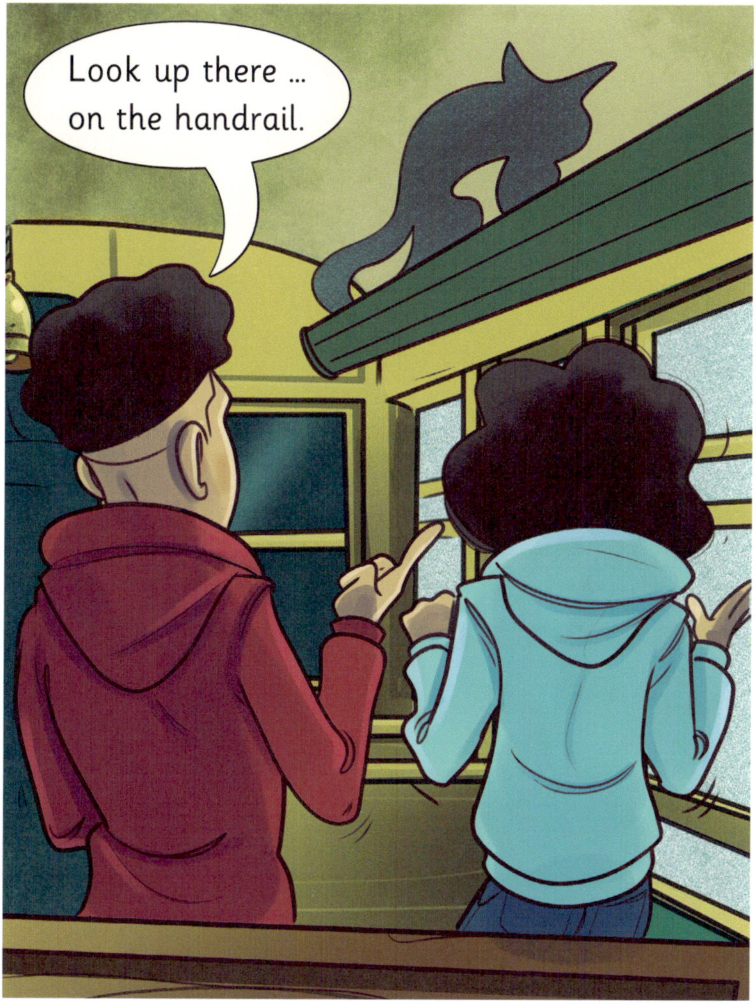
Look up there ... on the handrail.

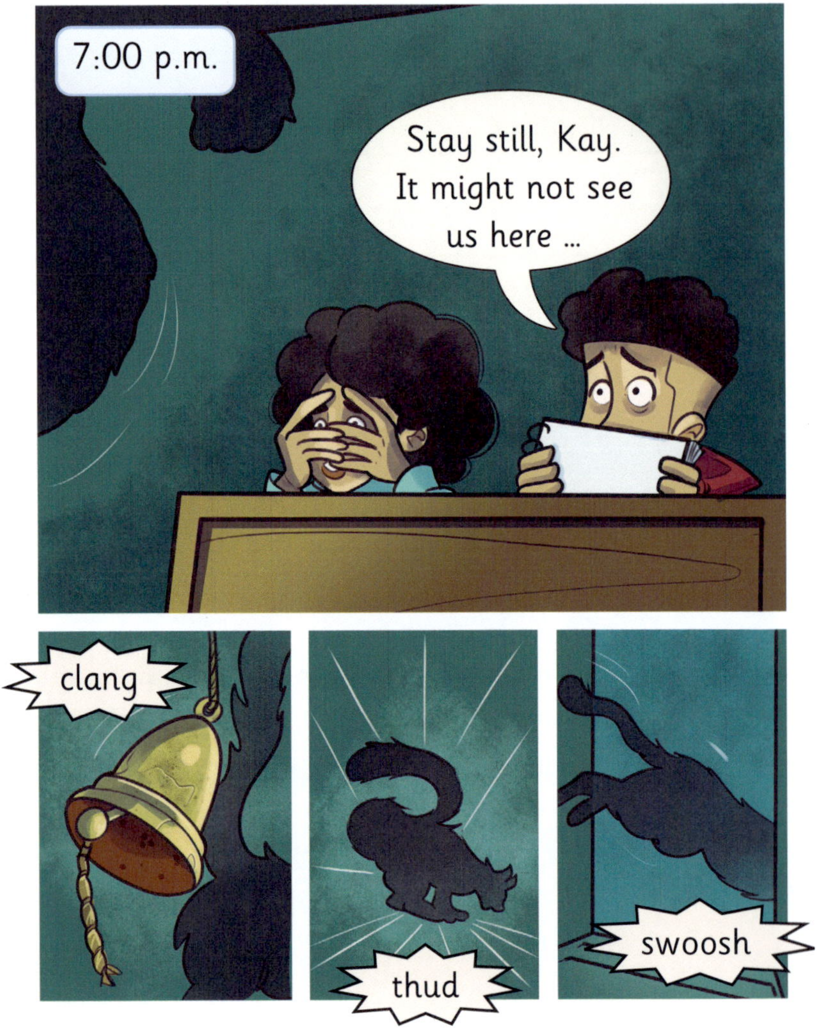
7:00 p.m.
Stay still, Kay. It might not see us here ...
clang
thud
swoosh

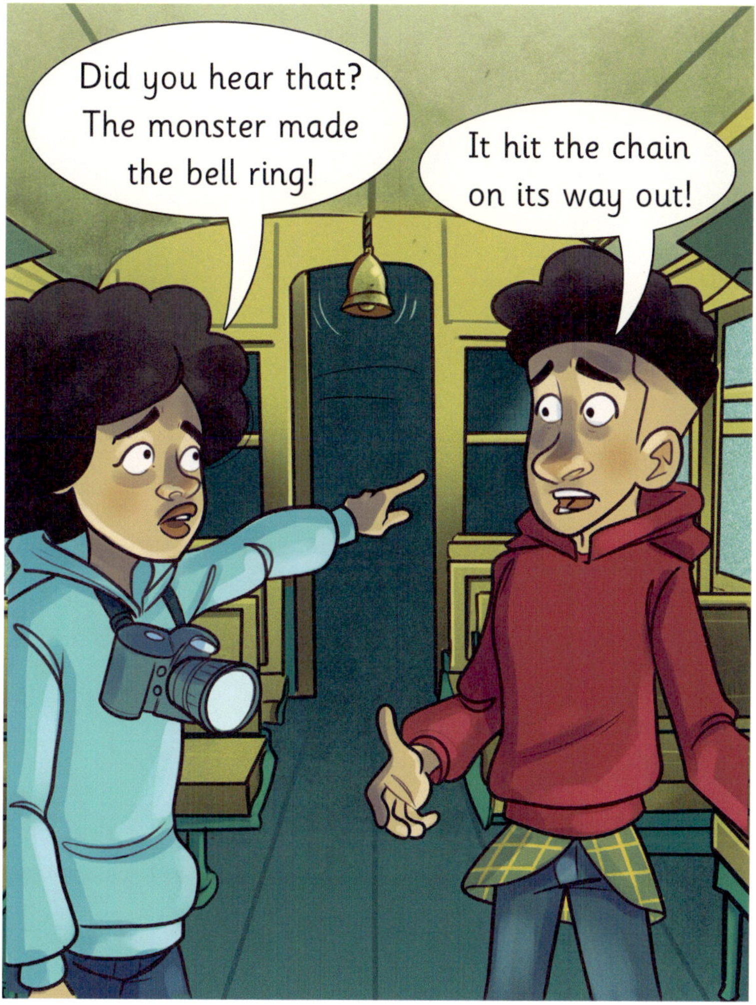
Did you hear that? The monster made the bell ring!
It hit the chain on its way out!

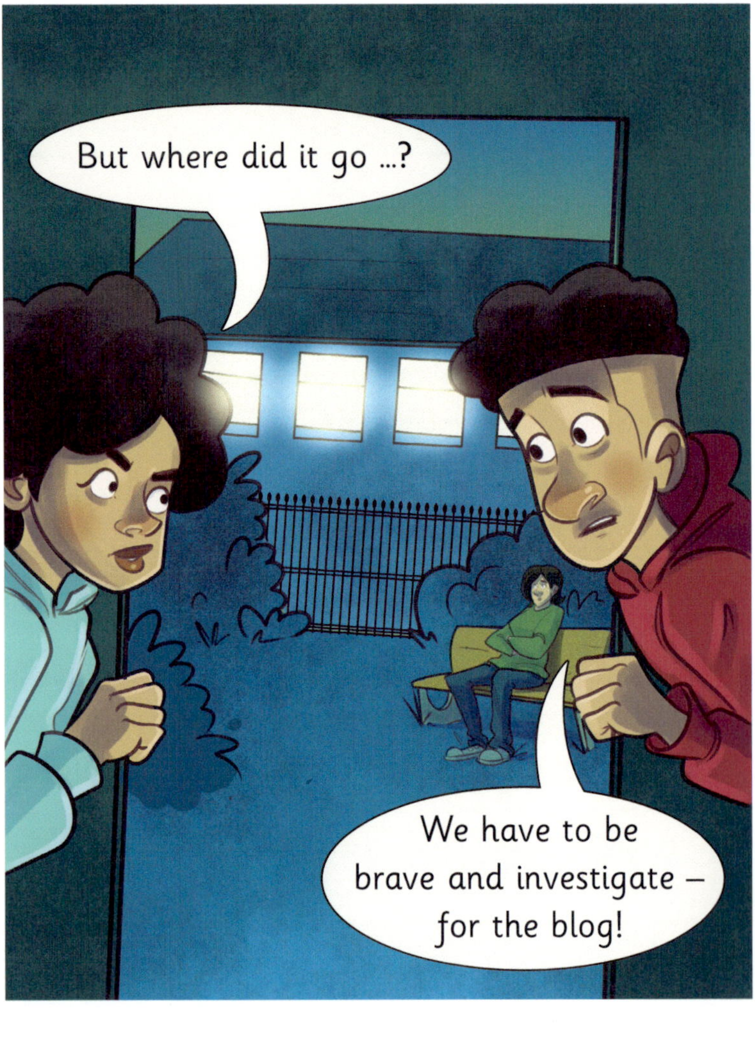
But where did it go ...?
We have to be brave and investigate – for the blog!

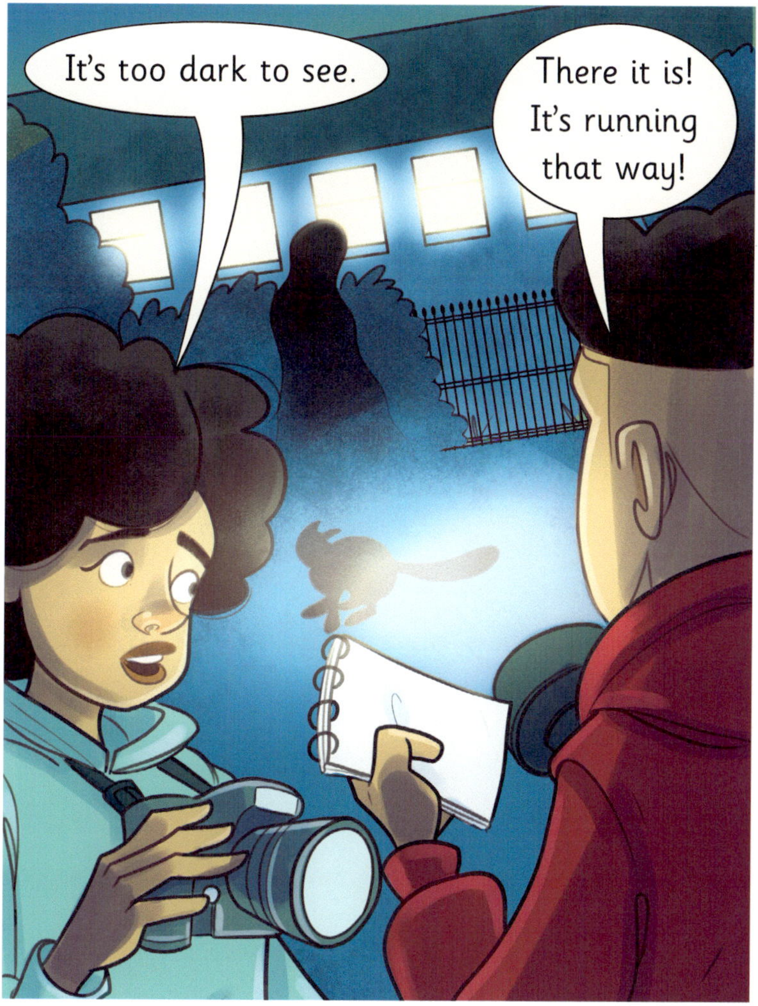
It's too dark to see.
There it is! It's running that way!

Chapter 4

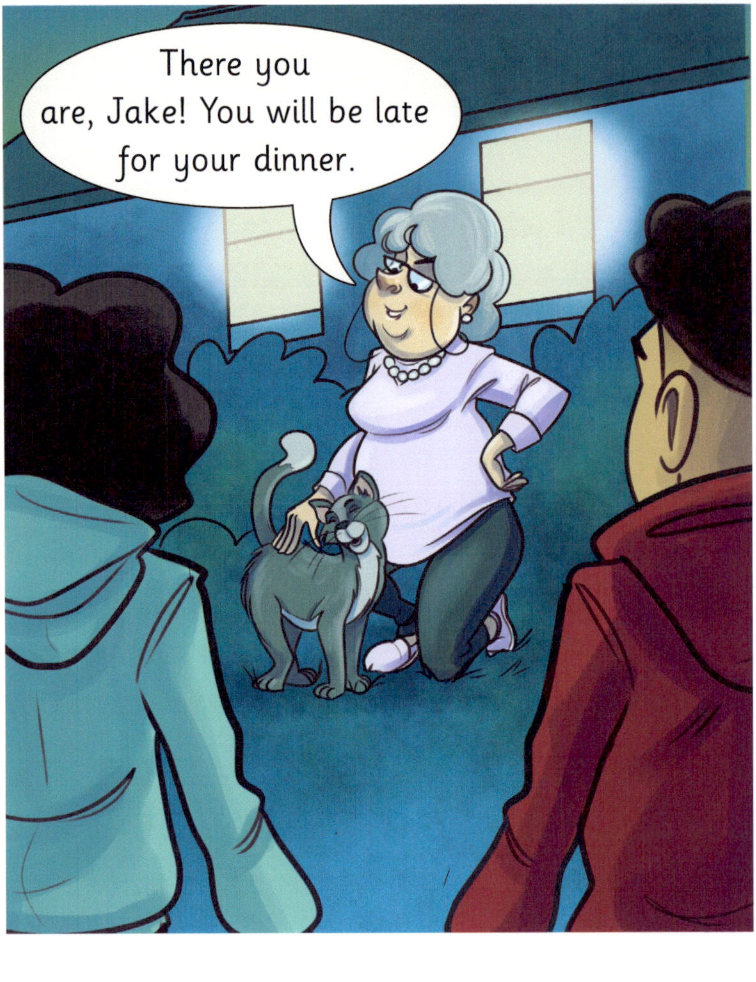
There you are, Jake! You will be late for your dinner.

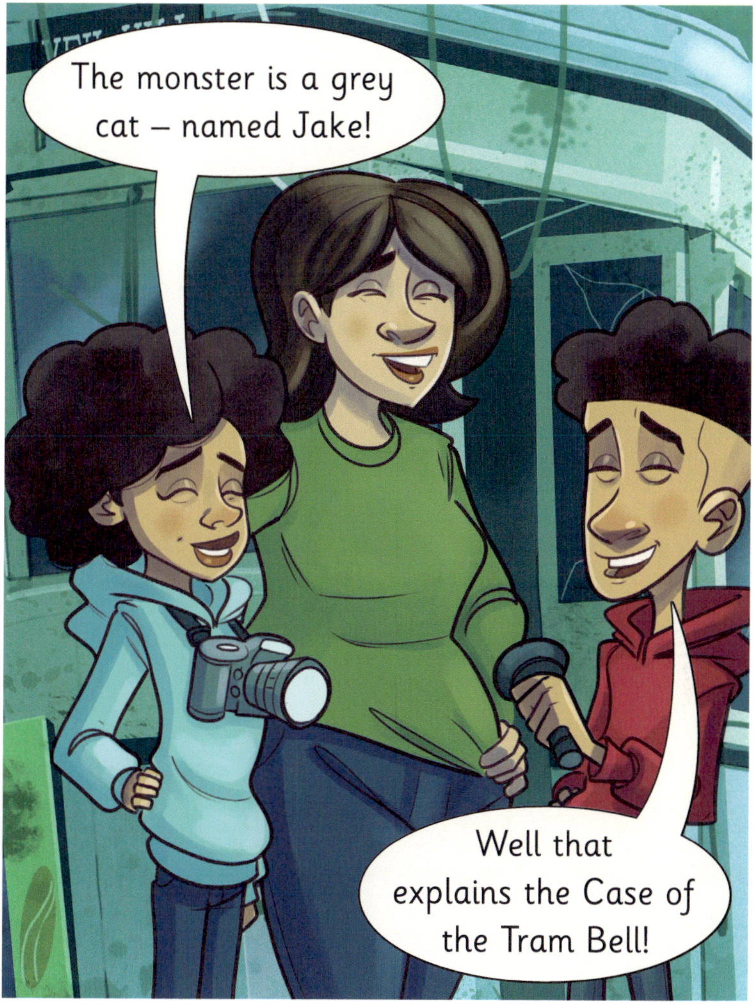
The monster is a grey cat – named Jake!
Well that explains the Case of the Tram Bell!

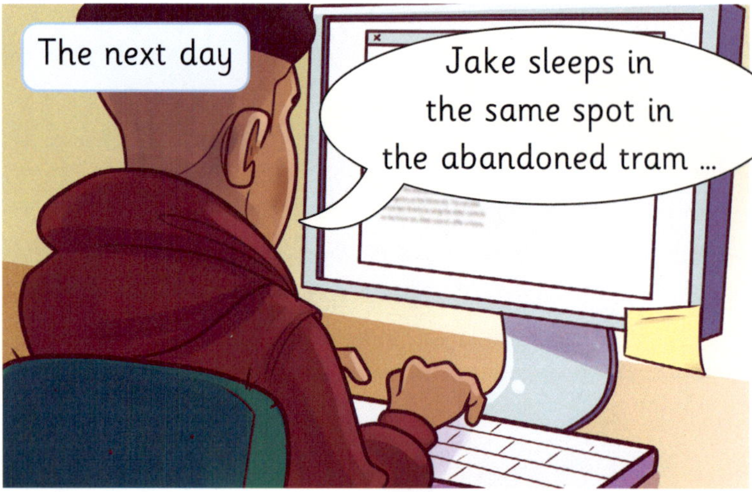
The next day
Jake sleeps in the same spot in the abandoned tram ...

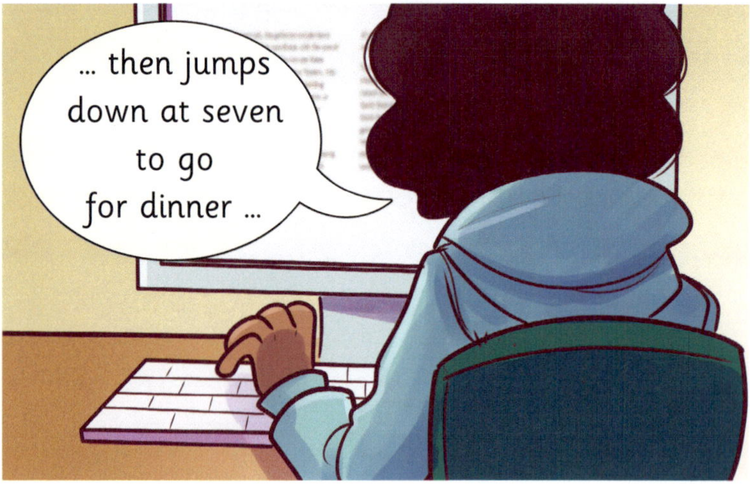
... then jumps down at seven to go for dinner ...

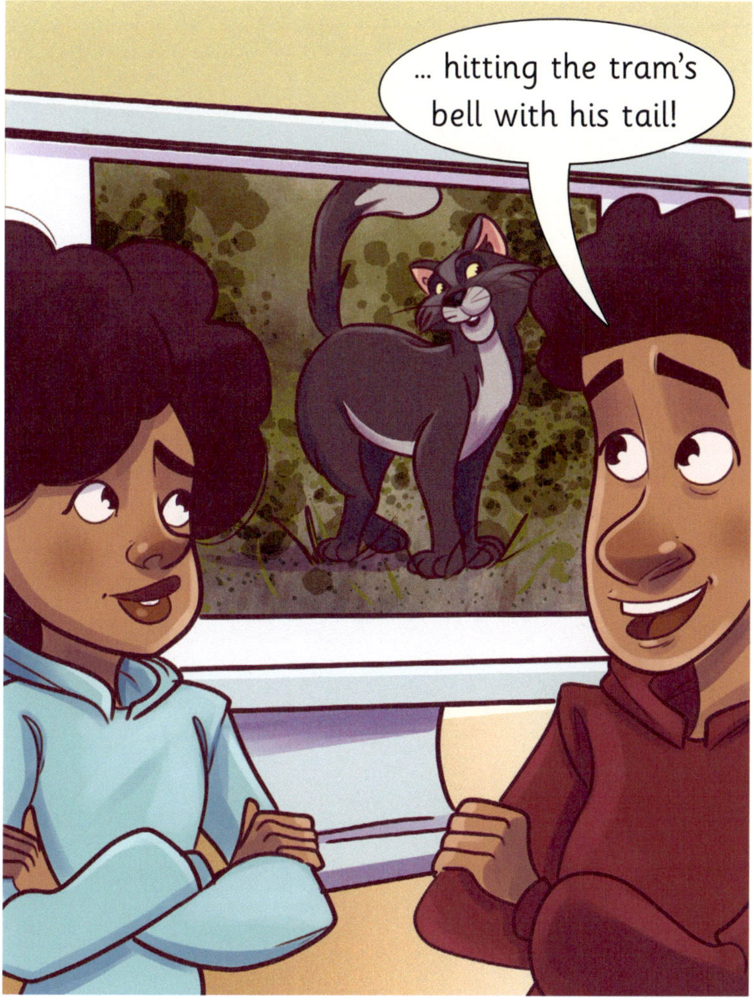
... hitting the tram's bell with his tail!

Published by Collins
An imprint of HarperCollins*Publishers*

The News Building, 1 London Bridge Street, London, SE1 9GF, UK

Macken House, 39/40 Mayor Street Upper, Dublin 1, D01 C9W8, Ireland

Phonemes covered:
/ai/ ay, a-e, ey, ei

Browse the complete Collins catalogue at
collins.co.uk

© HarperCollins*Publishers* Limited 2025

10 9 8 7 6 5 4 3 2 1

A catalogue record for this publication is available from the British Library.

ISBN 978-0-00-878607-6

All rights reserved. No part of this publication may be reproduced, stored in a retrieval system, or transmitted in any form by any means, electronic, mechanical, photocopying, recording or otherwise, without the prior written permission of the Publisher or a licence permitting restricted copying in the United Kingdom issued by the Copyright Licensing Agency Ltd, 5th Floor, Shackleton House, 4 Battle Bridge Lane, London SE1 2HX.

Without limiting the exclusive rights of any author, contributor or the publisher of this publication, any unauthorised use of this publication to train generative artificial intelligence (AI) technologies is expressly prohibited. HarperCollins also exercise their rights under Article 4(3) of the Digital Single Market Directive 2019/790 and expressly reserve this publication from the text and data mining exception.

Author: Carol Mitchell
Illustrator: Alan Brown (Advocate)
Publisher: Katie Sergeant
Product manager: Natasha Paul
Commissioning editor: Suzannah Ditchburn
Phonics consultant: Catherine Baker
Phonics reviewers: Rachel Russ and
Jacqueline Harris
Proofreader: Sally Byford
Original edition designer:
2Hoots Publishing Services Ltd
This edition designer: David Jimenez
Production controller: Katharine Willard

Printed in the UK.

This book contains FSC™ certified paper and other controlled sources to ensure responsible forest management.

For more information visit:
www.harpercollins.co.uk/green
collins.co.uk/sustainability

Made with responsibly
sourced paper and
vegetable ink
Scan to see how
we are reducing our
environmental impact.